I'll Follow the Moon

I'll Follow the Moon

the
Moon

Written by Stephanie Lisa Tara

Illustrated by Lee Edward Födi

BROWN BOOKS • DALLAS, TEXAS

I'll Follow the Moon
© 2005 Stephanie Lisa Tara
Original illustrations by Lee Edward Födi

Manufactured in Thailand.

For information, please contact:
Brown Books Publishing Group
16200 North Dallas Parkway, Suite 170
Dallas, Texas 75248
www.brownbooks.com
972-381-0009
A New Era in Publishing™

ISBN 1-933285-13-3
LCCN 2005928713
1 2 3 4 5 6 7 8 9 10

~For Aunt Barbara~
whose encouragement shines
as bright as the moon

Warm

Soft

Dry

I dream in blue.
Shimmering yellow,
And turquoise too.

I'm coming, Mama, I'll see you soon
I know just how . . . I'll follow the moon

Click
Clack
Tap

Blue melts away.
As I tap, crick, crack,
I spin, I sway.

I'm coming, Mama, I'll see you soon
I know just how . . . I'll follow the moon

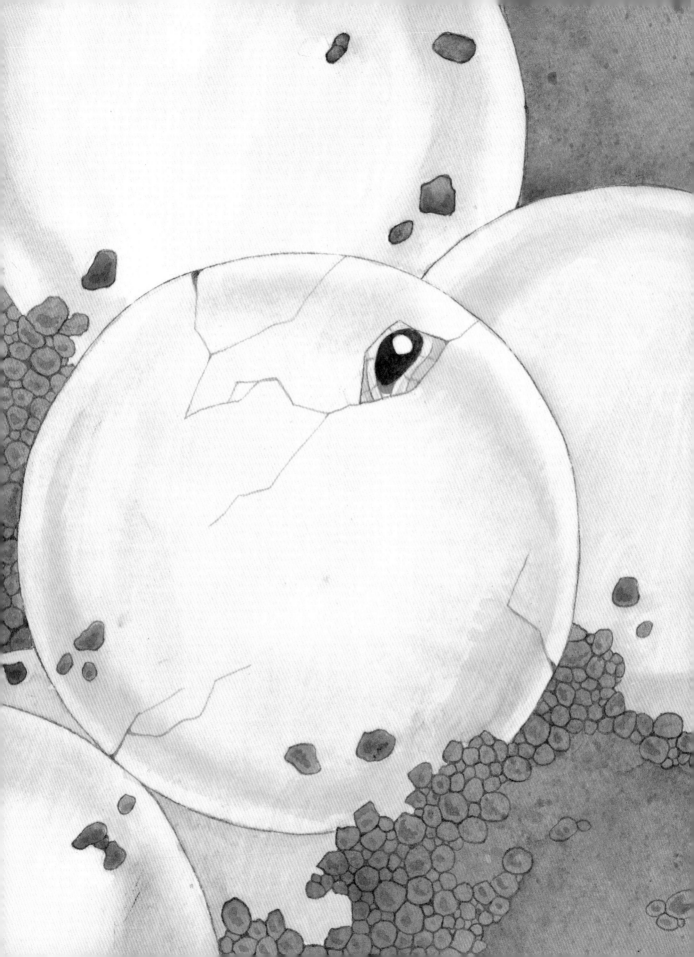

Roll
Slide
Tumble

I push, I shove.
Boom, bang, shake, and stop,
What is above?

I'm coming, Mama, I'll see you soon

I know just how . . . I'll follow the moon

Tap
Push
Crack

My beak breaks through.
A bit at a time,
All so new.

I'm coming, Mama, I'll see you soon

I know just how . . . I'll follow the moon

Out
Free
Lost

It's time to dig.
Through damp, sticky stuff,
Places so big.

I'm coming, Mama, I'll see you soon

I know just how . . . I'll follow the moon

Crawl
Scoop
Shove

My flippers glide.
From here, now to there,
They slip and slide.

I'm coming, Mama, I'll see you soon
I know just how . . . I'll follow the moon

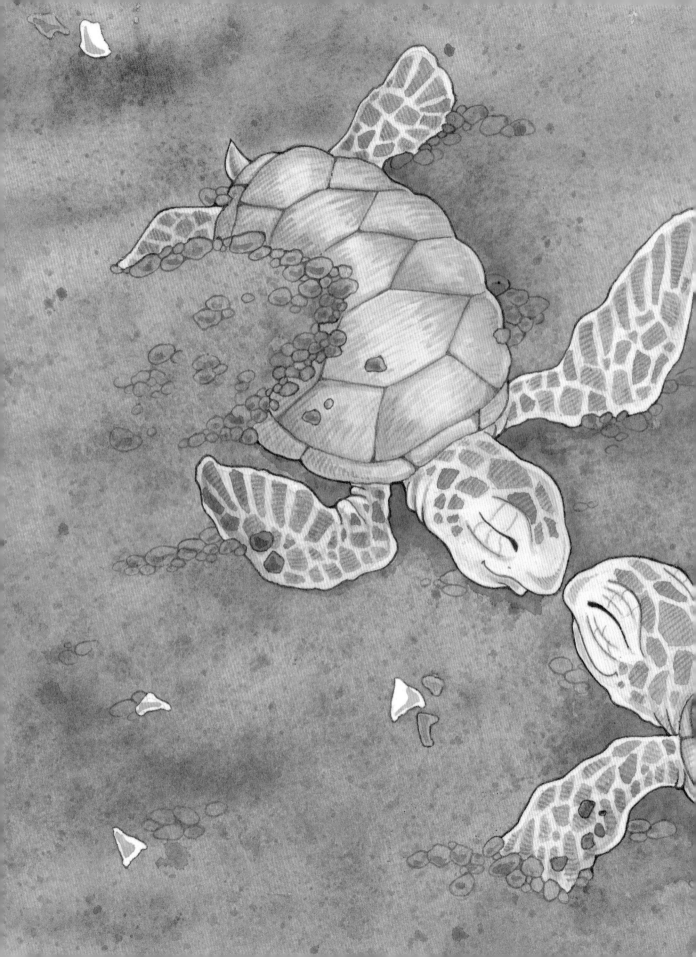

Oops You Too

Why, we're the same.
With flippers flapping,
A special game.

I'm coming, Mama, I'll see you soon

I know just how . . . I'll follow the moon

Up

Down

Around

Together, strong.
We each find a path,
It won't be long.

I'm coming, Mama, I'll see you soon
I know just how . . . I'll follow the moon

Whoosh
Night
Kiss

I breathe in deep.
Salt air on my face,
Turtle-heart leap!

I'm coming, Mama, I'll see you soon

I know just how . . . I'll follow the moon

Fine
Blue
Glow

Spill over me.
Oh moon, high above,
Eternity.

I'm coming, Mama, I'll see you soon
I know just how . . . I'll follow the moon

Stretch
Flex
Go

Under moon's sheen.
Stripes over my back,
Of deepest green.

I'm coming, Mama, I'll see you soon

I know just how . . . I'll follow the moon

Strong
Sure
Clear

Flippers move fast.
Moon sparkles my way,
Lights glitter past.

I'm coming, Mama, I'll see you soon
I know just how . . . I'll follow the moon

Wet
Spray
Tickle

Water on me.
Rushing, crashing sounds,
Much more to see.

I'm coming, Mama, I'll see you soon

I know just how . . . I'll follow the moon

Gulp

Spin

Float

I lose my place.
Water swirls me round,
Look for a face.

I'm coming, Mama, I'll see you soon
I know just how . . . I'll follow the moon

Swim
Look
Search

Moon knew the way.
Now here in my dream,
I wait, I stay.

I'm coming, Mama, I'll see you soon
I know just how . . . I'll follow the moon

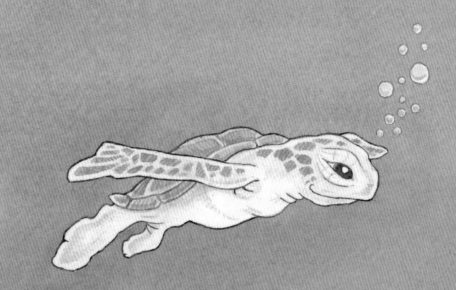

Eyes
Like
Mine

Of deepest blue.
Shell to shell we go,
In love, anew.

I'm here Mama—here with you
I knew I'd find you, Moon did too.

I'll Follow the Moon chronicles the journey of baby green sea turtles, nest-to-sea, exploring their extraordinary instinct to follow flickering moonlight home. Green sea turtle mothers deposit more than one hundred eggs in a subterranean beach nest, and after a two-month incubation period, the baby turtles hatch, dig to the surface, and crawl home to the sea.